KT-528-902

For Bertie MT

To Ralph and Lilo SA

Text copyright © 1990 Marilyn Tolhurst
Illustration copyright © 1990 Simone Abel

First published in Great Britain in 1990 by ABC

This edition first published in 1993 by softbacks,
an imprint of ABC , All Books for Children,
a division of The All Children's Company Ltd
33 Museum Street, London WC1A 1LD

Printed and bound in Hong Kong

British Library Cataloguing in Publication Data
Tolhurst, Marilyn
Somebody and the Three Blairs. - New ed
I. Title II. Abel, Simone
823.914

ISBN 1-85704-018-X

Somebody and the Three Blairs

Words by Marilyn Tolhurst
Pictures by Simone Abel

softbACks

FALKIRK COUNCIL
LIBRARY SUPPORT
FOR SCHOOLS

One Sunday morning, in a small house on the edge of town, a family was sitting down to breakfast.

There was Mr Blair, Mrs Blair and Baby Blair.

"It's such a fine morning," said Mr Blair, "I think we should take a walk in the park."

"What a good idea," said Mrs Blair.

"Feeda ducks," said Baby Blair.

So they took their coats and a bag of breadcrumbs and they set out for the park.

   While they were gone, Somebody came to the
door. Somebody knocked and, when no one
answered, Somebody tiptoed in.

He sniffed and sniffed.
He looked at the breakfast table.

"This food is too dry,"
said Somebody.

"This food is too noisy,"
said Somebody.

"But this food is just right."

He looked for somewhere to sit.

"This seat is too hard,"
said Somebody.

"This seat is too wobbly,"
said Somebody.

"But this seat is just right."

He looked for something to play with.

"This game is too noisy,"
said Somebody.

"This game is too cold,"
said Somebody.

"But this game
is just right."

He looked for something to drink.

"This rain is too hot,"
said Somebody.

"This pond is too small,"
said Somebody.

"But this stream is just right."

He looked for somewhere to sleep.

"This bed is too big,"
said Somebody.

"This bed is too small,"
said Somebody.

"But this bed is just right."

When Mr and Mrs Blair and Baby Blair came back from the park, they looked at the breakfast table.

"Somebody's been eating
my crunchies," said Mr Blair.

"Somebody's been eating
my crispies," said Mrs Blair.

"All gone!" said Baby Blair.

They looked around the room.

"Somebody's been sitting
on my chair," said Mr Blair.

"Somebody's been sitting
on MY chair," said Mrs Blair.

"Bust!" said Baby Blair.

They noticed the mess.

"Somebody's been emptying the cupboard," said Mr Blair.

"Somebody's been raiding the 'fridge," said Mrs Blair.

"Naughty!" said Baby Blair.

They went upstairs.

"Flood!" shouted Mr Blair.
"Help!" shouted Mrs Blair.
"Water!" shouted Baby Blair.

They looked in the bedrooms.

"It's a burglar,"
said Mr Blair.

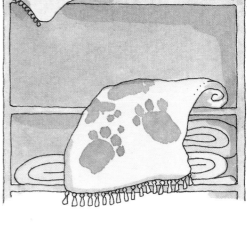

"It's a monster,"
said Mrs Blair.

"Issa big Teddy,"
said Baby Blair.

"It's escaped from the zoo," said Mr Blair.
"It's escaped from the circus," said Mrs Blair.
"Iss escaped downa drainpipe," said Baby Blair.

"Somebody phone the Police!" said Mr Blair.
"Somebody call the Fire Brigade!" said Mrs Blair.
"Somebody gone home," said Baby Blair.

FERNAME SUPPORT
FOR SCHOOLS

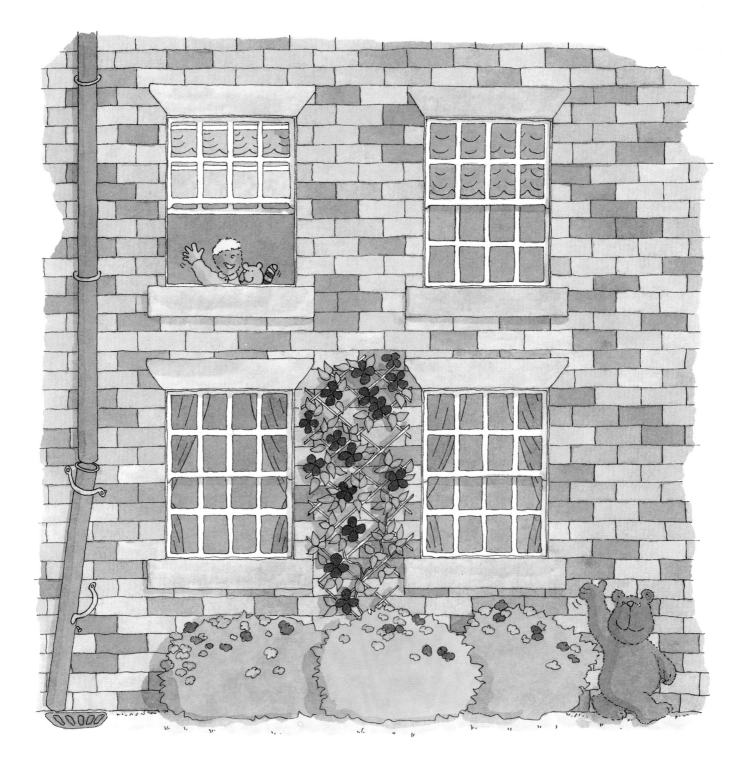

"Bye bye. Come and play tomorrow."

FALKIRK COUNCIL
LIBRARY SUPPORT
FOR SCHOOLS